A LITTLE SOMETHING

To my "Baba" Eva Krawchuk,
who gave me so much to remember her by.
SVB

To Kathleen Phillips, whose close bond with my daughter
echoes the one portrayed in this universal story.
LM

TCP Press
9 Lobraico Lane, Whitchurch-Stouffville, Ontario, L4A 7X5 Canada
(905) 640-8914, www.tcppress.com

Publishing Coordination: Brian A. Puppa
Design and Production: Douglas A. Bosak, V. John Lee
Printing and Binding: Friesens, www.friesens.com

The text is 16-point Goudy Oldstyle. The art was rendered using
watercolors and casein on a 100% rag, cold press surface illustration board.

Library and Archives Canada Cataloguing in Publication
Bosak, Susan V.
        A little something / Susan V. Bosak ; illustrated by Laurie McGaw.
Originally publ.: Whitchurch-Stouffville, Ont. : Communication Project,
        1997 under title: Something to remember me by.
ISBN 978-1-896232-06-5
        I. McGaw, Laurie II. Title.
PS8553.O7365S65 2008   jC813'.54   C2008-900574-0

Printed in Canada
14 13 12 11 10 09 08   8 7 6 5 4 3 2 1

A Little Something

Susan V. Bosak
Illustrated by Laurie McGaw

tcp

TCP PRESS · TORONTO

THEY ARE THE SPECIAL TIMES that make memories. Every time the little girl visited her grandmother, the house smelled so good. She and her grandmother would bake cookies together. It was always fun.

The house was happy on sunny days and cozy on rainy days. The little girl could have a snack anytime she wanted. She could use the big box of crayons in the kitchen drawer to add drawings to the pad of clean, white paper that was just for her. She could chatter about everything and ask questions by the dozen.

And if she spilled her juice, her grandmother would just wipe it up, saying that accidents happen to little people and big people. Then her grandmother would smile a big, warm smile and give the little girl a warm, snuggly hug.

THE LITTLE GIRL visited her grandmother often. Her grandmother always had time to play a game of cards – with cookies and milk, of course.

Sometimes grandmother and granddaughter would go for a walk together. They would see how many different kinds of birds they could find.

Sometimes they would go grocery shopping. The little girl could choose whatever she wanted her grandmother to cook for dinner.

Sometimes they would get ready for a party for friends and relatives. The little girl would figure out exactly the right place to put each shiny spoon and knife and fork.

Sometimes they would water the small garden at the back of the house, or pick beans or pull carrots.

AND SOMETIMES grandmother and granddaughter would just sit and watch television together.

The grandmother would get an apple and a paring knife from the kitchen. She would carefully peel the apple, letting the strands of red fall to the napkin in her lap. She would cut the apple in half, dig out the core, and slice big wedges for the both of them to munch on.

"You're the best grandmother in the whole world!" the little girl would say.

The grandmother would smile a big, warm smile and give her granddaughter a warm, snuggly hug.

AT THE END of one of the visits, the grandmother took her granddaughter's hand.

"I want to give you a little something to remember me by," the grandmother said as they walked into the bedroom. "Someday, that cedar chest at the foot of the bed will be yours. But for now, I want you to have this."

She handed her granddaughter an old wooden doll. It wore a pale yellow dress with white flowers on it. The painted face had bright red lips and big, wide-open eyes with long eyelashes.

AFTER THAT, many of the visits ended in the same way. Grandmother and granddaughter would go into the bedroom and the grandmother would say exactly the same thing: "I want to give you a little something to remember me by. Someday, that cedar chest at the foot of the bed will be yours. But for now, I want you to have this." Then the grandmother would give her granddaughter this or that.

As the girl grew, so did the number of things her grandmother gave her – a stuffed bear with soft, white fur; a carved wooden flute; a china figurine of a boy and a small puppy; a shiny, copper-colored coin with strange writing on it; a fancy pen that you had to use with special ink; a round, gold watch on a thick chain; a silver picture frame; and a flowery, orange and red and brown and blue tablecloth.

The tablecloth was the one thing the girl thought was *really ugly*. But she took it and said thank you as always.

ONCE, the girl asked why her grandmother gave her all these things to remember her by.

The grandmother smiled a big, warm smile and gave her granddaughter a warm, snuggly hug.

"Because everyone wants to be remembered," said the grandmother simply.

The girl didn't quite understand.

THE GIRL grew up into a young woman. She moved far away. But she and her grandmother would talk on the phone often. The grandmother would listen all about the young woman's work and about her new family. She was so proud of her granddaughter.

At the end of one telephone call, the grandmother told her granddaughter to watch for a package in the mail. The next week, a small box filled with tissue paper arrived. Nestled deep in the tissue was a handsewn cushion in the shape of a heart. It was stitched with big purple flowers, tiny pink flowers, and special lettering.

There was a note with the cushion: "A little something to remember me by."

THERE CAME A DAY when the grandmother made an important call to her granddaughter. It was time to come and get the cedar chest. The grandmother was moving out of her house.

The grandmother couldn't take care of the house any more. She couldn't see as well as she used to. She couldn't hear as well as she used to. Her hands didn't work as well as they used to. And she had trouble remembering some times and places and names.

So, the young woman came to get the cedar chest and to help her grandmother pack.

WHEN ALL THE PACKING was done, grandmother and granddaughter stood and looked at the empty house. The granddaughter was sad. The house was a very special place for her. The grandmother was sad too – but not about the house. It was time to leave the house. Something else was bothering her.

"I'm worried," said the grandmother. "I'm forgetting too many things."

"Everyone forgets things," responded her granddaughter reassuringly.

"But," said the grandmother softly, "I'm scared that… that I'm going to forget *you*."

The young woman was silent. She looked at her grandmother. She thought for a moment.

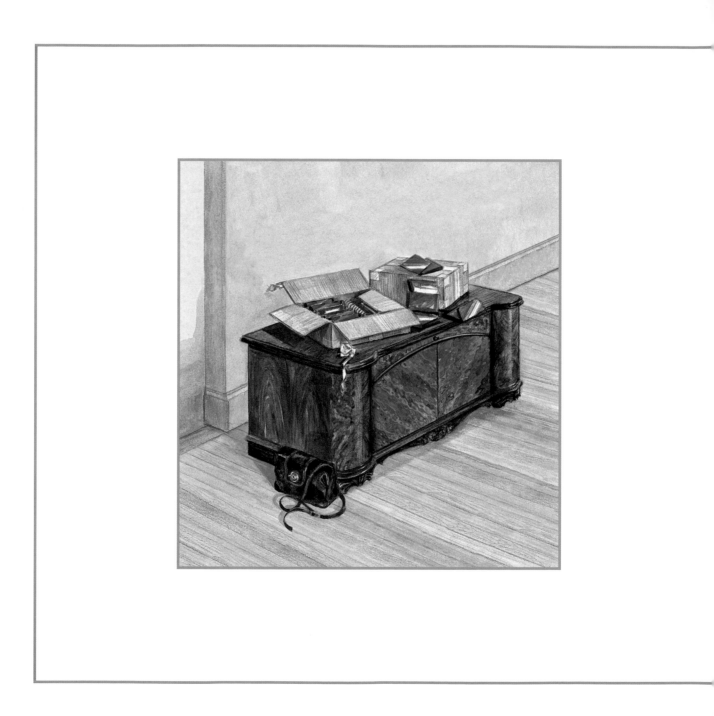

THE YOUNG WOMAN reached over to the boxes her grandmother had insisted go with them in the car. She ripped the tape off the top of one box and rummaged through it.

Finally, she found the photograph she was looking for – of grandmother and granddaughter. In big, bold letters, the granddaughter wrote both their names on the back of the photograph.

"A little something to remember me by," said the young woman as she handed the photograph to her grandmother.

The grandmother smiled a big, warm smile and gave her granddaughter a warm, snuggly hug.

TIME PASSED. The grandmother was very, very old. The granddaughter traveled once again to see her.

When the young woman walked into her grandmother's room, she expected a big, warm smile and a warm, snuggly hug, like always.

But there was only a blank look. The young woman put down the flowers she had brought. "It's me. It's your granddaughter," she repeated, not believing her grandmother wouldn't remember her.

The grandmother looked confused. The young woman sat down by the bed. She talked to her grandmother while she was awake. She held her grandmother's hand when she fell asleep.

THE GRANDMOTHER'S HAND was small and wrinkled, but it was soft and warm. The granddaughter stroked the hand and she whispered, "You're the best grandmother in the whole world."

The grandmother opened her eyes. And then, for a moment, she smiled that big, warm smile!

The grandmother lifted her granddaughter's hand toward the drawer beside the bed. The young woman opened the drawer.

Inside was the old photograph of grandmother and granddaughter. The edges were tattered and one corner of the photograph was bent. The writing on the back was smudged.

THE YOUNG WOMAN went back to her home, her work, and her family. The cedar chest sat in her bedroom, at the foot of the bed. The chest was filled with all the special things the grandmother had given her granddaughter.

The young woman knelt beside the chest and opened it slowly. She looked through the contents. She could almost hear her grandmother's words, "I want to give you a little something to remember me by."

But the young woman's heart really didn't need any of the things to remember her grandmother. Her grandmother had given her much more than would ever fit in the cedar chest.

As the young woman glanced up from the cedar chest, she noticed her reflection in the dresser mirror. She got up and went to the mirror.

She looked closely. She looked for a long time.

And then she smiled a big, warm smile – her grandmother's smile.

Legacy

PAST I PRESENT I FUTURE
WWW.LEGACYPROJECT.ORG

Explore and celebrate the special legacies in your family – the memories, keepsakes, traditions, stories, and life lessons passed from one generation to the next.

The Legacy Project is a multigenerational education initiative. Its Across Generations program, in partnership with Generations United in Washington, DC, helps you bring the generations closer in your family and community. Get free online resources and activities that children, parents, and grandparents can do together, from family tree charts to a fill-in generations scrapbook to keepsake crafts.

Other books include the award-winning bestseller *Dream*, illustrated by fifteen top children's illustrators, which inspires children and adults with its poetic story about hopes and dreams throughout a lifetime. The popular grandparenting guide *How to Build the Grandma Connection* offers practical tips and ideas for building family bonds, even over long distances. The Legacy Project also offers the annual Listen to a Life Contest, the Life Statement Library, workshops, and traveling exhibits.

Find out more, 1-800-772-7765 or www.legacyproject.org.